ALSO BY LOUISE GLÜCK

POETRY

Firstborn

The House on Marshland

Descending Figure

The Triumph of Achilles

Ararat

The Wild Iris

Meadowlands

Vita Nova

The Seven Ages

Averno

A Village Life

Poems 1962–2012

Faithful and Virtuous Night

Winter Recipes from the Collective

ESSAYS

Proofs & Theories

American Originality

Marigold and Rose

Marigold and Rose

A Fiction

L OUISE G LÜCK

F ARRAR , S TRAUS AND G IROUX

N EW Y ORK

Farrar, Straus and Giroux
120 Broadway, New York 10271

Library of Congress Cataloging-in-Publication Data
Names: Glück, Louise, 1943– author.
Title: Marigold and rose / Louise Glück.
Description: First edition. | New York : Farrar, Straus and
    Giroux, 2022.
Identifiers: LCCN 2022022852 | ISBN 9780374607586
    (hardcover)
Subjects: LCGFT: Novels.
Classification: LCC PS3557.L8 M37 2022 | DDC 813/
    .54—dc23/eng/20220518
LC record available at https://lccn.loc.gov/2022022852

Designed by Gretchen Achilles

Our books may be purchased in bulk for promotional,
educational, or business use. Please contact your local bookseller
or the Macmillan Corporate and Premium Sales Department
at 1-800-221-7945, extension 5442, or by email
at MacmillanSpecialMarkets@macmillan.com.

www.fsgbooks.com
www.twitter.com/fsgbooks · www.facebook.com/fsgbooks

1 3 5 7 9 10 8 6 4 2

For Emmy and Lizzy

Marigold and Rose

MARIGOLD AND ROSE

Marigold was absorbed in her book; she had gotten as far as the *V*. Rose didn't care for books. She particularly disliked books of the kind Marigold was presently reading, in which animals substituted for people. Rose was a social being. Rose liked activities in which people figured. Like baths. She liked being soaped all over by Mother or Father and then being rinsed until she was spotless. Usually something would be exclaimed on. Her silky skin. Her beautiful eyes with their dark lashes. But to be left out as she was now, to be unnecessary—this she did not like. I am not just spotless, she thought to herself. I am also stripeless.

Marigold was still reading. Of course she wasn't reading; neither of the twins could read; they were babies. But we have inner lives, Rose thought.

Marigold was writing a book. That she couldn't read was an impediment. Nevertheless, the book was forming in her head. The words would come later. The book had people in it but it also had animals. All books, Marigold felt, should have animals; people were not enough.

Marigold knew this was utterly alien to her sister, just as Rose's eager sociability and curiosity, her calm self-confidence, were alien to Marigold herself. This must be why they were twins. Together they included everything.

I will put that in my book, Marigold thought, when things did not go well for her.

She felt she would never be perfect as Rose was. Who's my good baby, Mother would say at mealtime. Rose could drink out of a cup. For the most part,

Rose was the answer. Next to Marigold's name there were a lot of needs improvement boxes checked. Marigold was not good at the cup. Milk spurted out of her mouth all over her bib.

Books did not judge you, Marigold thought, perhaps because they were full of animals. She knew from the dog, animals did not judge you.

Rose missed her sister. Marigold was there in the playpen but Marigold was not there. These were hard times; Rose was lonely. She understood that Marigold was resourceful and she was not. She was a good baby but she was not resourceful.

Soon it would be naptime. Outside the playpen there were day and night. What did they add up to? Time was what they added up to. Rain arrived, then snow. We needed rain, people said. But no one said we needed snow.

At the other end of time your official life began, which meant it would one day end. This came to

Marigold in a flash. I will be grown up, she thought, and then I will be dead. I miss my sister, Rose would say. I must write her a letter.

You have become quite a letter writer, Marigold would tell her. And she would smile in her little room. And Rose, so far away, would see that smile in her mind's eye. Being gregarious, as she was, didn't preclude having a mind. Marigold had explained it.

You must learn to trust people, Rose would say. The more you trust, the more you can afford to lose. You must swell the ranks, she said.

Turn the page, she thought in the playpen. Turn the page. She could see the zebra, striped as it always was. How dull, she thought. And Marigold turned the page, not because Rose told her but because she wanted to.

Sharing with Bunnies

Before the bunnies came there was a beautiful garden filled with all manner of flowering things. The things were all white; Mother was not prone to color. White tulips underplanted with Virginia bluebells. It was spring. Summer was different; there was not enough sun once the trees leafed out. The garden relied on nasturtiums, which Mother and Father ate. It was strange to see the grilled fish with nasturtium butter melting over it. The twins only knew because Mother told them.

But once you try, Mother said, the taste is magic. The twins knew what magic was. It made the sun rise. Now they knew it had a taste, which was the taste of flowers. But only this particular flower. Others you must stay far away from. This seemed very confusing. Best, Marigold thought, to stay far away from the garden lest you get too close to something dangerous blooming.

Mother and the twins were sitting on the blue blanket. The twins thought Mother was lovely. She had enough hair so it went in many directions when the wind blew. Father was splendid. You are lucky girls, Mother said, to have a handsome father; you should try your best to look like him. She said nothing about herself. People with good manners didn't talk about their own attributes. This was called blowing a horn.

Mother had paused in her weeding. She was sitting with the twins on the blue blanket that was kept in the shed for exactly this purpose. Nostalgically the twins had their heads in her lap. The heads bumped from time to time. Long ago—this is what they remembered.

It was a beautiful day. Mother had said so. Father was off counting things.

Mother did not spend a lot of time on the blanket; she was energetic and purposeful. This must be why she had twins, Marigold thought, instead of a regular baby. It was known Father had wanted a goldfish. The twins watched from the blanket. It was still safe there; they couldn't as yet crawl.

In their different ways they loved this period. It was possible still to feel safe. They didn't know this was what they felt until the feeling disappeared, though initially they were distracted, like all babies, by feelings of triumph. First crawling, then walking and climbing, then talking. Their clothes stopped fitting. Pajamas with feet were no longer appropriate. Infinite possibility—something they both felt. Then an absence or loss. Safety, which had disappeared. But all this was still to come.

Meanwhile, the nasturtiums were gone. If you strained your eyes you could see the beheaded stems. But the riot of color was nowhere to be seen. Rose and Marigold didn't know this; they had never seen a riot of color. This would have been their first.

Mother was kneeling down, then standing up. Mother was struggling, Rose could see, to master her distress. She is trying to be calm for us, Rose thought, so we will be calm. Marigold, she thought, is prone to agitation. Take a leaf from my book, Rose thought, though she couldn't say so.

Mother was walking the garden, taking note of the bald places. The twins waited for her on the blanket. Rabbits, she said, when she sat down at last. They are in a book, Marigold thought, but they were called bunnies. That must be their name for children. And she longed, once again, for adulthood with its vast cargo of words.

Mother sat on the blanket. She will talk to us about sharing, Marigold thought. Mother was committed to sharing, as she told the twins. The twins didn't like to share. They each wanted everything all the time. It was the same with Mother. She didn't want to share the garden with the bunnies, but she knew she must even if the reason wasn't completely clear. Nevertheless, she put wire cages over the few surviving nasturtiums.

Time to go in the house, Mother said. The sun was setting. It was going to be a beautiful summer day once, and now it had been a beautiful summer day, so it was time to go home.

The twins were in the playpen, smelling the warm smells of inside the house. Father was coming home. Drums in the twins' hearts. He would pick them up, each one in turn, and lift them high into the air.

We are thriving, Rose thought; Rose was sensitive to the moment. And Marigold thought this was true, she who took the long view.

Marigold's Dream

Marigold was dreaming the dream she dreamed. She was a single baby; Rose was nowhere to be seen. Perhaps she had decided not to be born. Beautiful Rose, lovable Rose. Because if she had been born she would surely have belonged to someone, surely Mother and Father. She was the sort of baby people would rush to claim and then hurry home with before the other parents could see her.

Marigold was not that sort of baby. Marigold was difficult. Well, life was difficult, she thought.

Life was difficult: finally you figured out how to climb the stairs. Unimaginably high, those stairs. Each stair came up to her waist. She would lean with her two arms on top of the stair, and then with great effort hoist herself up on her hands and knees. And then have to stand up and repeat the whole thing. I learned, Marigold thought, and then I fell to the bottom. Rose was looking down at me.

But that was not in the dream. Sunlight was in the dream. And that successful feeling that in Marigold's waking life eluded her. Then how did she know how to feel it in her dream? And she could talk: that she remembered.

Meanwhile the dream, which should have continued pleasantly, was beginning to be permeated with misery and fear. She must have done something to Rose to make her not be. And it was true: she had hit Rose; once she stuck her finger almost in Rose's eye. Rose often hit Marigold and stuck her fingers wherever they could go. But that Rose would have these dreams was impossible.

Whenever Marigold looked, there she was, sleeping soundly in her crib, often smiling in her sleep. I must have inherited Jewish guilt, Marigold thought. It was inherited from Father. Father had the full complement of Jewish guilt though he was only half Jewish. At least this was what he said.

Then it was morning. All in all, Marigold was glad of morning. Rose was making a lot of noise. Really all the noise; Marigold smiled at Mother when Mother arrived. And later she ate her oatmeal from a spoon. She even held the spoon like a real person and not a baby.

Mother and Father understood that Marigold envied Rose. (Poor little Rose, thought Mother. Poor little Marigold, thought Father.) But Rose adored her sister. People have pets they love, but Rose had Marigold.

And while it was true there was a little condescension in these feelings, possibly even pity, it was also true that under this there was a deep regard, an admiration for a being felt in some way to be superior. At least less diffuse (as social beings are diffuse).

As though the sweet puppy had become the service animal, or even the Seeing Eye dog, on whom life depended. There was in Rose, despite her obvious beauty and great charm, a deep vein of humility, born, she later felt, of her love for her sister, a reverence slightly touched with awe, as though to Rose Marigold was a kind of prophet or holy figure.

Marigold, she saw, was dreaming her dream. She had pulled off all her blankets. And Rose felt a painful wish to restore the blankets and stroke her sister's damp hair, but of course this was impossible, owing to the bars of the crib.

THE CHILDHOOD OF MOTHER

Marigold's book had a name; it was called *The Childhood of Mother*.

About this subject, little was known. But a book had to have a name, just as Rose and Marigold had to have names before anything could happen to them.

Rose was perennial. This meant she was always there, in her one place, just getting bigger, whereas Marigold was annual. You seed yourself, Mother said; this seemed to her a cheerful fact. But Marigold did not think it was cheerful. For one thing, it meant she was homeless, never knowing where she would be from one year to the next, maybe another garden entirely, without Mother and Father to carry her around when she was tired. You are a multitude; Mother said this also. It meant that though you might have one rose in your garden (what a marvelous rose, people would say), you would never have one marigold. I cannot think, Marigold thought, why they would have done this to me.

Who am I, she thought to herself. Or really, which am I of the hundreds in the original packet. This was not a question Rose would ever need to ask. But it explained the book: Marigold needed something that stood for herself as Rose stood for Rose.

How little we know, Marigold thought. It was known that Mother was once a little child and Grandmother was her mother. Before that she was a baby, though not so little as the twins were. The twins were really one baby divided by two. I am half a baby, Marigold thought. I am the brain and Rose is the heart. Or was it the other way? Father had also been a baby though he was always a boy. Other Grandmother was his mother. Other Grandmother lived far away; the twins did not know her.

Who took care of us, Marigold thought, if Mother was a baby? But the twins couldn't as yet ask questions. They had to take what they could pick up, like pigeons in the public park. Still, Mother was what Marigold knew best, aside from Rose. But she couldn't name the book *The Childhood of Rose* because Rose hadn't had a childhood.

How little we know, Marigold thought again. She decided she would say what the twins did and then she would change their names to Mother. You can't do that, thought Rose. You should only tell a true story. It is true, Marigold thought; it just isn't real.

But the book was very slow because the twins didn't do anything. They lay in their cribs, behind bars like criminals. Sometimes they went to the park. They liked the infant swings. They liked the slide too, but only if Father kept them sitting up, one hand on their backs and one hand on their fronts. But the sliding the twins did. They also used real spoons. They could both drink out of cups. They could crawl and stand up if they had something to hold on to. Rose could say "bear." Would people who could read be interested in this?

Mother and Father, Marigold thought. They would be interested.

And Rose thought, Not if you change our names.

It was hard to see into Rose's mind, or hear what went on there. Marigold could hear her own thoughts without any trouble, but she heard nothing from Rose's head, not even when their heads were close. Maybe because of the hair, she thought. Or maybe Rose was hard to hear because she had no turbulence.

So it was strange that Rose talked first. Never jump to conclusions, Mother said. This meant you never knew what would happen. Mother thought this made life interesting. Father didn't say what he thought. You had to watch to know. He's like me, Marigold thought.

Rose was watching her sister. What an odd little thing she is, Rose thought. All her energy is in her head. And then she thought, I have known her since before she was born. And because she was worldly, it worried her to think what other people would make of Marigold. And then, because she was like her name, steadfast and true, she united herself with her sister, as though they were a single story to which Mother and Father were just witnesses.

FORWARD MOTION

Mother and Father were thinking of buying a house. Or rather, Mother was thinking of buying a house and Father was going along. This was what he did; he went along and then he just stopped. The twins knew this. Mother seemed to know it too; she would study his face to see if the stopping thing was coming over it, and then, if she thought it wasn't, she would plunge ahead. Mother believed in forward motion. And the twins felt Father profited from this; in any case, he sometimes got caught up in it and would sail ahead like a surfboarder riding a wave.

Father inherited the stopping thing from Other Grandmother, who was famous for it. But the twins were like Mother. In one year they had gone from being tadpoles that didn't know how to breathe to being actual miniature people, able to drink out of cups and make many different sounds and climb the stairs on their hands and knees though they were still in diapers. Nevertheless, it had to be admitted that Marigold would sometimes pause at the top of the stairs to look down with her meditative gaze at where she had been. And she had been known to sit down on the top step, which was increasingly nerve-wracking since the stairs stayed the same size but her bottom didn't.

When Mother discussed the house she said the twins didn't fit into the apartment. Maybe she was thinking about Marigold and the stairs. But they did fit; it wasn't as though the elastic broke or the snaps didn't snap anymore. There weren't any snaps. There were just rooms and bathrooms and beds and cribs.

Though the twins thought of Mother and Father as a single unit (as the twins were a single unit) it was important to remember that they were separate people with separate needs and preferences, just as the twins were. And they had separate names too, just as the twins did. Mother stressed this in her many conversations with Marigold and Rose about how to live life.

Though Mother was committed to pushing forward, she was a big believer in planning ahead; she didn't like surprises. Father didn't like surprises either, but the stopping thing pretty much protected him. Nobody in the family liked surprises.

Meanwhile, Rose was talking more and more. Well, not talking exactly since she didn't bother about words. But she was definitely doing something very similar, in loud gusts and torrents. This is because she likes people, Marigold thought. Marigold did not like people. She liked Mother and Father; everyone else had not yet been properly inspected. Rose did like people and she intended them to like her. I would not have believed she was capable of such volume, Marigold thought. It was a great surprise, that volume. Rose looked more likely to have a gentle murmur, so that people would lean close. She wants them to see her eyelashes, Marigold thought.

Apparently, Rose was no longer concerned with her eyelashes. She was shouting because she was angry and she was angry because no one understood a word she said. Just like a teenager though in actual fact she remained a baby, with round dimpled silken arms.

Now every day was like the days when the twins did not perform well at naptime. Then Mother and Father would begin to look tired and harassed. Mother explained that babies got tired too; often, they cried because they were tired. I don't cry because I'm tired, Marigold thought. I cry because something has disappointed me. Strangely, given the violence of her conversation, Rose was not much of a crier. I have higher standards, Marigold thought.

Sometimes she thought she might just skip talking altogether, and wait for writing.

In their different ways, the twins were beginning to remember. They remembered different things. Or they remembered the same things differently. How could you know? But it did not come easily. It seemed to Marigold that you remembered things because they changed. You didn't need to remember what was right in front of you. And the twins were still too little to have much behind. But Marigold wanted to be prepared for change, which meant you had to learn to remember before you needed to remember.

What do you think, Rose, said Marigold. What do you think, Marigold, said Rose.

Marigold stood at the top of the stairs, looking backwards to where she had been. She held on to the gate that was just ahead so that she wouldn't fall. It seemed to her a very long way she had traveled. Then she crawled over the threshold.

Long, long ago: that was how she would begin her book.

But actually it was Rose who remembered farther back, being the older twin. I will have to breathe first, Rose thought (it was her first memory). I will have to teach her.

Rose and the Elephant

All of a sudden, Grandmother went to Heaven. This was not like when Father went to work. For one thing, when you went to Heaven you went there and stayed there. For another thing, according to Mother, Heaven was known to be wonderful. It was a distant place where people you loved went to be happy. Even Rose thought this was questionable. The twins were beginning to understand that there was a particular kind of explanation they thought of as explanations for babies. How this differed from not telling the truth wasn't clear. But you knew you had gotten one of these when Mother said, One day you girls will understand.

They didn't, as it happened, understand. And they didn't believe Grandmother was happy. Grandmother loved babies; she especially loved the twins. No one talked about whether there were babies in Heaven. But the twins knew that as far as Grandmother was concerned they were the best of all possible babies so they couldn't believe she was happier in her new home. Also Mother said it was full of light. The twins knew that made sleep hard and Grandmother had told them how hard sleeping was for her already—the twins felt this as a special bond.

During this period, Mother was very sad. That was the word Father used. He told the twins Mother was very sad because she had lost Grandmother. But Mother knew exactly where she was. Not only that: she had regularly explained that because we still thought about her all the time, Grandmother was not lost; she was still baking cookies in the twins' hearts.

Mother also reminded them that Other Grandmother was still with them. But she wasn't with them. She was also in another place though that place had

airplanes. But Other Grandmother was not interested in the things babies were interested in. Father
had noticed this too, when he was a baby.

It was dawning on the twins that this might be a sig-
nificant problem with grandmothers. Sooner or
later they were going to live far away. They would
stop being available to comment favorably on things
the twins had or did, like their dimples (they both
had dimples) and sweet-smelling skin.

It was also around this time that Mother began to
talk about going back to work. She told Father that
she wanted to contribute to the household. If you
asked the twins (no one did) they would say that
Mother contributed by being Mother. Father explained that to Mother this was different because
mothers didn't get paid and apparently people who
got paid contributed and people who didn't get paid
were no help at all. The twins saw right through this.

But Mother decided it was worth trying, and Father
didn't stop her. He said you had to let people find
their own way. So one day Mother got dressed in

clothes and kissed the twins and went out the door. This was a lot of going away in the twins' lives all at once.

It was not a happy time. This was the first the twins understood that word, *happy*, but they understood it because it was gone. Like the way they understood remembering (this was Marigold's thought). Marigold was sensitive to diminishment, being the smaller twin. They had always been happy it seemed and now they were not. (It was not known how they felt in the incubator but at that time they were not yet themselves, twins, because they were not finished.)

As it turned out, Mother changed her mind about work. She decided she would try again when the twins were older. This seemed connected to the earlier idea about understanding Heaven, which would also happen when the twins were older. It did not make being older seem like a good thing. Rose reminded Marigold that Father went to work and nobody seemed upset. But Father had always gone to work, so the twins were used to it, and besides there was always a festival when he came home.

Mother was home but the twins knew somehow they were getting older whether they wanted to or not. They would someday walk instead of crawl. They would have teeth. And the diapers would be gone, along with Grandmother and the apartment, though the stuffed bear would still be with them wherever they were; it would follow them as it had followed Father. And if the stuffing came out it would get new stuffing.

Everything will disappear, Marigold thought.

It was evening. Rose was smiling placidly in the bathtub playing with the squirting elephant, which, according to Mother, represented patience, strength, loyalty and wisdom.

How does she do it, Marigold thought, knowing what we know.

Everything will disappear. Still, she thought. I know more words now. She made a list in her head of all the words she knew: *Mama*, *Dada*, *bear*, *bee*, *hat*. And both these things would continue happening: everything will disappear but I will know many words. More and more and more and more, and then I will write my book.

ONCE TIME

L*ong, long ago*, Marigold wrote. And then she stopped. I am Father all over again, she thought. Which she was, the Mother half being largely silent. It will come later, Rose said. She had lots of the Mother half but lived in hopeful expectation of waking up one day to find Father had surfaced in the night. That would be the way, she thought.

Marigold stopped because she did not know where to go next. But perhaps you never knew, Marigold thought. Greatness, she felt, would not come easily to her.

You cannot help what you dream, she said, to no one in particular. But really of course to Rose, who was the only person she could talk to since they did not as yet use words.

None of this was written down. But it was taking shape in her head, all day it seemed. In the twins' room darkened for naptime, in the bathtub and stroller, while Rose yelled loudly at the world, like a schoolchild demanding to be called on.

How could it take shape without words? Marigold didn't know. Perhaps it was an offshoot of some ancient form, from that wordless time before Greek or Sanskrit. In any case, it had her in its grip.

Marigold was a strong-willed baby who had overcome great odds, given how little she was when she was born. But what was happening was not willed. Of that she was sure. This was why she trusted it. She could never, naturally, trust herself. She trusted her book, but even so she was having problems.

Marigold was having second thoughts. Not new thoughts. Questions about her old thought. She had loved *long, long ago* (being a twin, she liked things that happened twice) but she had become aware of another way to begin, a way Mother and Father both used when they read stories at bedtime. *Once upon a time*: that was what the stories said. The sticking point was *upon*; neither Marigold nor Rose had any idea what this meant. Mother and Father never used this word, except when they were beginning books. Mostly it was Father who used this. When it was Father's turn at bedtime, he often chose *once upon a time*; Mother usually chose *long, long ago*. He would say the words slowly. And he explained the hard ones, like *upon*. *Up*, he said, and *on*. He picked up each twin in turn and held her up (saying the word) and then put her on (usually Mother and Father's bed). Mother and Father had one bed but the twins each got a private crib.

Despite Father's efforts, Marigold never quite got the hang of the word. She had a good grip on *once* because she heard *one* in it, which was how Father and Mother would begin counting lessons (holding up their fingers). And time was the difference between waking up and going to sleep; it was how you got from one to the other. *Once* must mean that time didn't happen again. Marigold once fell down after sliding and scratched her face and had to have both Band-Aids and kisses. Never again would she have those same Band-Aids or tear the pink sweater with the white heart in that same place.

Once time, Marigold repeated to herself, leaving out the *upon*. She was trying to hear what the book wanted. Then she listened and waited. But the book was completely silent in that way of nonexistent things. I will wait as long as I have to, Marigold thought. When the book is ready to talk it will talk. Like us, Marigold thought. Like Rose and me.

THE WINGED SOUL

Everyone understood that Marigold lived in her head and Rose lived in the world. Well and good, Rose thought. Living in your head looked very nice to someone out in the wind and rain (this was Rose on a bad day). It all adds up, she thought later. Meaning all the solitude adds up, all the concentration on invisible things, trying to make them visible. It adds up to wind and rain, she thought. But certainly it seemed attractive now, when the twins were babies.

Rose knew how to smile at strangers. She was why the twins got red lollipops at the doctor's office instead of the yellow other babies got. And she knew these things without being taught. Father, who had painfully mastered this smiling at strangers through long years of hard work, often marveled at Rose. It amused him to wonder if the fruits of hard work could be passed down genetically, though in reality hard work disappears with the worker.

In most other ways, Father was more like Marigold, though without her literary obsessions. He had not tried, in infancy or any other time, to write a book. Even later, when he acquired words, he felt nothing like Marigold's passionate yearning. But the temperament, the propensity to stop or to refuse, to buy time you might say: in this Marigold was his duplicate. My little mirror, he used to call her. And she would smile at him in her way. Provisionally.

Nevertheless a person meeting him would have said he resembled Rose because he was handsome and good with people. (This was before Rose started to talk.)

But Rose knew otherwise. Even Marigold, with her nose in a book, watching the bear change to a cow and then a donkey, even Marigold knew that Father was nothing like Rose.

Rose found this painful. She loved being like Mother but she felt not being like Father as a real lack. Being like Father would add depth and variety to being like Mother. Rose felt sometimes that she lacked depth. She felt a little one-note, like a highly decorative cave painting.

She listened to Father carefully when it was his turn to do baths or bedtime. How soothing he was, even washing the sore parts, as though he knew what being sore felt like. You expected this with Mother, whereas with Father it was a surprise because he was so quiet as a rule. This sort of surprise, this multi-dimensional quality, was what Rose meant when she thought about her own limitations. Marigold gave no thought at all to these matters. And now, since she had started talking, Rose felt she was turning into a tyrant. And Marigold was quieter than ever, training herself to keep the green pencil inside the outline of the frog, studying the alphabet book for clues.

Rose knew better than to think this staying inside the lines was Marigold's life plan. Marigold had understood since she was very little (really very, very little) that it was necessary to acquire the discipline of staying inside the lines before you began the great work of drawing outside them.

I understand her so well, Rose thought. And then, a little sadly, much better than she understands me. Unlike Rose, unlike most babies, Marigold did not live in the present. Her soul has wings, Rose thought (she was not entirely lacking in metaphoric insight). And the thought pleased her greatly; it seemed almost like something Marigold might have thought. And she wanted to tell her sister this and decided that one day she would, once she knew words.

THE GOOD PROVIDER

Your father is a good provider, Mother said. The twins felt this was true: he had provided Mother. And after a little while, Mother provided the twins. We are a perfect match, Rose thought.

Mother and Father each had a special baby. Not that they had labels: Mother could perfectly well diaper Marigold, and Father was admirably natural when he burped Rose. But everyone knew Rose was Mother's baby and Marigold was Father's. Or maybe it happened the other way. Maybe Rose took Mother, being the one born first, and Marigold got Father. Rose took no time at all to deliberate. This was her way.

Or maybe Father paired up with Marigold because the burping took her such a long time and Father was more patient. Also it was well known that Mother had more on her plate. Father just had wine on his plate.

In other more final ways, Rose had Marigold and Marigold had Rose. This was their secret.

Sometimes of course Rose wanted Father, and in the same way sometimes Marigold desperately needed Mother. There were even times when both twins wanted both parents and then calamity ensued. This often happened after their shots or when they were teething.

Neither Mother nor Father knew the first thing about twins when they started to have them. Mother and Father were expecting two of the same baby, like a double order in a restaurant. Or maybe what you found at a department store, the same dress in different sizes. But from the very first no one had any trouble of this kind.

At the moment, Rose was learning to talk. Marigold was learning to watch. She was an excellent watcher.

Whatever is she looking at, Rose would often think. She seemed to be seeing things Rose couldn't see, even seeing a Rose Rose couldn't see.

How did people know this about Marigold? They knew. It was that look she had, Rose thought. Her important baby look was what Rose called it.

She is the thinking one, Mother said. Rose was the everything else one. But everything else doesn't count, Rose thought. And Marigold thought everything else was everything. Because you couldn't *see* thinking.

But she did think. And she felt things. The alphabet book affected her deeply. Each letter had its own page. Then in the end they teamed up to make the alphabet. In other books, this alphabet could fall apart to make words, any word you could think of. The unused letters seemed to Marigold tragic and gallant. But they all had jobs to do sooner or later, making *kangaroo* and *zebra* and *bear* and *pigeon*. And this gave Marigold hope, which she often needed, given how quick she was to expect the worst.

None of this made the slightest bit of sense to Rose. Even as a dream, it didn't make sense. And sense was Rose's middle name.

And what was Rose doing while Marigold was dreaming her dream? Rose was staring at her new feet which had purple bows in the middle of them. Rose was very pleased. They were not feet anymore. They were shoes.

Marigold and Rose
Are One

Suddenly one day the twins were turning one. *Become*, Mother said. They had become one. What was become, Marigold wondered. It meant they were once not one and then they were one. But what was not one? Nothing, Marigold thought. We were nothing.

It was a happy day. There were balloons on the ceiling. There's going to be a party, Rose thought. How did she know?

But the twins could not become one if they'd been one before. Which they had been, Marigold knew. Long ago, when they were an egg.

It was unlike Mother, who was usually so reliable and well informed, to tell them two facts that couldn't both be true. Even Rose, who was distracted by the approaching party, could see something fishy was going on. We have to go along with it, she thought, being mainly concerned with self-preservation and only occasionally interested in accuracy or truth.

Becoming one meant the twins had completed one of every month and all the days inside the months. All these months together added up to one. Now they could begin on the two of every month that would add up to two.

I don't understand, Marigold thought.

Meanwhile though they were presumably one now there were two cakes, cupcakes to be exact, one for each twin. And there were candles. Mother and Father blew them out but soon the twins would be able to do that themselves, and make wishes also. Everyone knew how that would go.

Everyone knew everything about everyone. That was the definition of family. Rose and Marigold and Father and Mother were a family. Two of them and two of us, Rose thought. She was partial to symmetry.

Rose was licking the last of the pink frosting off the cupcake top and was beginning on the cake itself. This she smashed into tiny glittering yellow crumbs; you could use them, she discovered, to make designs on the tray part of the high chair, which she was happily doing with whatever crumbs were not already on the floor. How adaptable she is, Marigold thought, with a certain resentment. Go with the flow, Rose thought.

Marigold did no such thing. She looked grimly out at the party from her high chair. Chaos and imprecision, she thought. Grown-ups were milling about. Grandfather had made a special trip. Meanwhile people they didn't know were touching them and calling them lambs and chickens though it was perfectly obvious they were human babies. Aging human babies, Marigold thought.

Then it was time to go home except for the twins and Mother and Father who were home already. It was night outside. The balloons were slowly floating toward the floor. They are tired, Mother said, just as the twins were tired.

It was night. For Rose, it had been a memorable day. Still she was sad that Marigold had liked so little about the party. But parties, she believed, had a special importance to people like Marigold who had important projects in mind. You could have a party in your book, she told her sister. It would be a way to get more people in, so more things could happen. It would even, she thought to herself, make a nice ending. End on a bright note, she thought, as though that were a good or even a possible thing.

That's a terrible ending, Marigold thought, though the good end eluded her. I am only one, she thought. I cannot even talk yet. I expect too much of myself, she thought. Whereas Rose who expected nothing did everything perfectly. Rose was an accomplished baby.

But a party was a terrible end, even if Rose liked it. And Rose, who had long ago given up defending her ideas and settled into a peaceful deference, kept brightly suggesting new ideas that anyone who gave any thought at all to books would know immediately could not possibly work. Then why not just have us go to bed, she said, which is what we always do. And in fact they did go to bed and to sleep, though in the book, of course, because of the name change, it would be Mother going to bed, with Father.

Really, Marigold thought, when the superfluous people had gone, it was much too soon to think about the ending. And Rose, in her own crib, agreed. Much, much too soon.

It was night, the night of the birthday, but Marigold couldn't sleep. *Long, long ago*, she said to herself, trying to make it real. And when that didn't work she tried the other way, *once time*, but that wasn't the answer. Rose was sleeping in her crib, making her little purring sounds and Mother and Father were sleeping in the big bed, just as they did in the book.

Except it isn't the end, Marigold thought. It's the beginning.

Deep, deep in the night. Marigold was having a dream. How happy she looks, thought Rose, who was now awake because it was her turn to keep the watch. It must be a wonderful dream.

And indeed it was. In the dream, Marigold was writing her book, a real book that people who could read would read. And nothing could stop her, even words couldn't stop her. All night she wrote. She wrote and wrote and wrote and wrote. The end was the morning.

I think I must have read that somewhere, Marigold thought, later the next day. But of course she couldn't have since she couldn't read.

Acknowledgments

Special thanks to Keith Monley, whose wry comment I stole for my first sentence: this book would not exist without him.

To Kathryn Davis, whose criticism has shaped this work and whose books have been its inspiration, an unrepayable debt.

To Noah and Priscilla, gratitude and love and pride.